The Eccentric and Feral

Alaric Maison

Published by Alaric Maison, 2024.

THE ECCENTRIC AND FERAL

First edition. January 8, 2024.

Copyright © 2024 Alaric Maison.

ISBN: 979-8230581222

Written by Alaric Maison.

CHAPTER 1

Jasper Hayes Novak.

The owner of the business card Evan was currently holding.

A photographer, huh? Did they usually have cards like this?

It wouldn't be right to leave it lying on the sticky club floor. That was Evan's only reason for picking it up, of course. It couldn't be because of the one who usually stood in that spot, right?

The one who always brought him back to reality when he was escaping his job and indulging in what this place had to offer. Maybe 'brought back to reality' wasn't exactly it, but that's what it felt like.

He stood out significantly among the other clubgoers. He never danced or anything like that. Just stood there. Observing.

Wearing that long jacket over a dark blue shirt, while his dark and longer-than-average hair framed his face.

Speaking of; why was a person matching that exact description walking in his direction?

Below blinding lights, the man's eyes swept the area. Was he searching for something? Oh right, a certain someone's card still lingered in Evan's hand.

The man glanced at it before their eyes slowly met. He was still standing a fair bit away, but the smile that parted his lips was both visible and alluring. There was a hint of recognition on his face. Their eye contact only lasted a few seconds, before the stranger turned his back to him.

Brought out of his temporary daze, Evan clutched the business card. Why was he leaving again? Wasn't he going to get the item back he lost?

A sudden hand on his shoulder made him freeze up, as he looked to his right for the culprit. Blonde, a bit shorter than him, and clearly up to something.

"That guy is definitely... interesting. Not bad though."

A soft, but weirdly endearing voice.

Had these two ...?

Seeing the blonde's gaze drift further down, Evan shoved the card into his pocket. Whoever he was; it could wait. Evan's reason for being here was just to get some cute guy's attention after all. And that goal had officially been accomplished.

"Not bad, huh? We'll see if I can compare, then."

"Ooh, now we're talking."

He ran his hand down Evan's arm, making him shiver.

It was going to be a good night...

It was quiet. Too quiet. Evan's one-man office, in all its extravagance, never did quite enough to make up for the endless amount of tasks he had to deal with.

Everything was blurry. All he could feel was his boss watching his every move.

On the large mahogany desk in front of him stood a laptop, its screen glaring in his direction. The calendar was packed as usual, but he knew it wouldn't take long before someone pestered him to add more to it.

That kind of despair was enough to force his mind toward better things—anything that was more tolerable than this. Like good memories of the only place he really felt at home. And no, that wasn't his top-floor apartment, as hard as he had to work for that one. No... the place he had a chance to get a glimpse of 'him'.

Digging through his pocket, he pulled the card out. Maybe he should take a small break and look at the website on it...

Artist biography, availability, client information, etc. Oh, and a link to his portfolio. Evan enjoyed the purple and green colors that were used for its smooth layout. A shame those didn't carry over to the page that opened up in front of him. Jasper's portfolio. The site was filled with images of men. Every single one looked different from the others. Interesting angles and all kinds of compositions. Sometimes there were multiple guys in one photo and other times there were tools involved. Often; both.

Despite the content, it was surprisingly tasteful.

He hadn't noticed how red his face was becoming before a familiar shape made its way into his office. The slam of the door when it closed made him sit up in an instant. That was the quickest he had ever changed tabs. And just in time too.

"Hmm... I usually don't look like that when I'm working. Did Erwin send you the wrong thing?" A coworker of Evans decided it was appropriate to sidle up behind his desk. Usually, he never allowed others to do that, but Will was the exception.

"You know he'd never make a mistake like that." Though there was some embarrassment in Evan's voice, he was often good at hiding undue emotions.

"I suppose you're right." Will scanned the computer screen, looking for anything out of place. Oh no, he was smiling now.

"What's tha-?"

"Nothing. Can't I have things running in the background that aren't related to work?"

"Mhm, right. I know someone who wouldn't be too pleased with that."

"Screw him."

"Woah, hey." Will laughed, as he continued.

"Anyway, I am here to make you aware of some emails that have been sent by our dear boss."

"Ah, just what I needed."

"Of course, of course. And isn't he generous? Sending me to make sure you got them?"

Evan fixed him with a sharp glare.

He checked it, and sure enough, there they were. Three new ones.

"What a lovely guy."

The sarcasm didn't go unnoticed. Will smiled, as he headed for the door, glancing back at Evan. With another slam of the door, he was left in silence once again.

His thoughts returned to the faces of those men on the bright screen. But also, the man who never seemed to be in focus or ever showed his face. His hair was familiar.

The photographer doesn't always stay behind his camera, does he?"

Despite the many neon lights the downtown area had to offer, they only did so much to help Evan navigate the streets. If anything, most shapes were only grazed by their soft rim light.

In front of the building he was walking towards, two men were leaning against the concrete. Smoke shrouded one of them; emitted by the cigarette between his lips. All Evan could tell was that they were talking. He was unable to identify any of their words. His attention was already taken by a much more mysterious-looking pair.

There they were. They?

Two shadows. Someone was with him and their voices were only mere whispers.

It didn't take long before they both slipped into a nearby back alley positioned between the club and its neighboring building.

Curiosity was getting the better of him. Could it be related to what he had seen on the website?

That thought was all the motivation he needed. With a quick look around himself, he disappeared into the dark.

"I don't understand. What do you mean 'no'? Isn't the customer always right or something?" An erratic voice. Impatient and pushy.

"Excuse me? You... You think I'm going to prioritize that over my own limits? That's not going to happen."

A recognizable stranger and a not-so-familiar one. The former had his back against the wall, eyebrows drawn together.

"I'll go slow..."

"No."

The man's piercing gaze shifted from the one in front of him to Evan. He had been spotted.

"Ugh. Whatever." There was something unnerving about his shakiness. But when he stepped away from the other guy and hurried out of the alleyway—past Evan—his heartbeat was able to settle.

"Asshole..." The man who remained pushed himself off the wall. As he made eye contact with Evan, he spoke up again.

"Oh, it's you. Here to give me my card back?"

"Actually..."

Just that hesitation alone made the man's lips curve up.

"I'm guessing you assumed I had more?"

"That's... part of it. Jasper, was it?"

"Yours truly."

Jasper closed the distance between them, as he continued. Evan's heartbeat spiked in an instant.

"So... I'd love to know what still made you want to talk to me."

Jasper pressed his fingers gently against the white fabric of Evan's dress shirt. Right where it stretched a little, as it tried its best to cover his chest. He was having a tough time keeping his eyes solely on Evan's face.

"There was just... something about your photos." Evan took a deep breath, as the stranger's hand inched further down.

"Was there also... someone?"

"...Maybe."

"Well... that someone has an apartment very close by."

"Does he now?" Reaching up for the hand on his chest, Evan grabbed Jasper's wrist.

What he had seen on the website represented this man well. Jasper had that kind of presence that made you want to be vulnerable around him.

"Mhm... you'd love it."

"I doubt I'll have much time to enjoy the interior."

"Oh my..."

CHAPTER 2

Only dim artificial lights decorated the entrance hall. However, not a single one hung from the ceiling. Jasper liked his darkness, it seemed. Images he recognized lined the walls, adding to the intriguing atmosphere.

Not that he had much time to consider it all, as he was shoved against said wall by a pair of surprisingly strong hands.

"You care about who's on who?"

"No."

"Perfect..."

As Evan climbed onto the bed, he saw Jasper walk in another direction. With his back to Evan, he rummaged through a dresser that stood right below a black part of the otherwise white bedroom wall. It had hooks scattered across it. On them, a large assortment of leather and metal 'devices'.

He didn't get more time to observe it, as Jasper sauntered toward the bed, familiar necessities in hand.

"Don't give me that look. That's where the budget goes."

Evan chuckled, re-examining the nearest parts of the room. There was a clock on the wall above him, and a blindfold lying on the nightstand beside him. It didn't have any drawers, which explained Jasper's need to get the lube and packets from somewhere else.

"Hey, I mean, your bedroom is both big and has all of this. I can admire dedication like that."

"Why, thank you." He emptied his hand onto the bed, before getting on it himself. As Jasper straddled his lap, Evan unbuttoned his own shirt and pulled it off.

Their eyes met. With a subtle smile, Jasper dropped his jacket on the floor before getting his shirt off as well.

A surprisingly athletic body... though something covered it still.

"Not bad... for an artist. I wasn't sure it was you when I saw those pictures."

"Oh, I see. You're gonna be like that, are you?"

Evan's smile widened. He traced Jasper's collarbone with his finger, curious. What hugged Jasper's bare skin was something quite unlike the bulldog harnesses he usually saw. It was a lot more intricate. The straps framed his chest nicely, while even more thin layers of leather wrapped around his waist.

"I'm so very sorry." Those words didn't hold any weight. Intentionally, of course.

"If you keep up that attitude, I'm tying you to the bed and edging you for the rest of the night."

"Is that a promise?"

Jasper grabbed the hand that was still by his collarbone and pressed it down onto the mattress. He then swiped his blindfold off the nightstand and twisted it, holding the fabric over Evan's lips.

"Anything else you need to get out before I close that pretty mouth of yours?"

That, without a doubt, made Evan's blood flow directly to his cock.

"Ah, just... Make sure to really get that frustration out. I want to feel it."

"Oh, I plan to." Jasper pressed the cloth in between Evan's teeth, wrapping it around his head, before tying a knot. However restrictive the blindfold may be, it felt soft on Evan's tongue.

Now that he wasn't getting distracted anymore, Jasper made quick work of fully undressing them both. He rolled the condom down and slathered himself in lube, spending no time loosening Evan up before shoving his cock deep inside him.

Evan's eyes shut tightly as he quivered against the disheveled bed sheets. He could feel impatience in the way Jasper moved. But considering what he saw earlier, it made sense that he was in a bit of a state. Also, that meant it wouldn't take long until...

"Nngh-"

Evan bit down on the fabric in his mouth—as his body convulsed.

Jasper was reaching it already. Every thrust after it was aimed right at the spot that made Evan whimper the loudest.

There it was. The feeling that dominated all others. It was a euphoric state to be in and one that always stopped his thoughts from wandering. It demanded all of his attention.

There simply was no better way to escape life...

The sun only got through one sheet of glass, as it made contact with Evan's face. The few other windows the room contained were blocked by large blackout curtains.

With a grunt, he sat up and rested his back on the headboard. It still hurt after last night, but the mild pain was manageable. Exactly how the morning after should feel. At least, according to him.

Evan smiled to himself, as he watched the other man sleep peacefully next to him. How was he allowed to look that good even when he wasn't fully conscious?

Though every muscle in his body protested, Evan still made it out of bed. He picked his boxers up off the ground and got them on.

It wouldn't be right to disrupt Jasper, so he opted to check out the apartment some more. Looking around, he noticed a camera and a desk located in separate corners near the door. Was he too distracted back then to see those?

It looked like Jasper had combined both a studio and a bedroom into one. It was charming in a way.

He surveyed the images that hung around him in the bedroom. There was something about their larger size and the amount of detail you were able to see. They were hanging so shamelessly on the wall.

As he walked through the room, he couldn't help but admire it. This place carried a lot more sentimentality than his own.

Slipping past the open door, he ended up back in the hallway. There were three doors apart from the one they came in through. Two of them were already opened, one leading to the kitchen, and the other, to the bathroom.

Curious, Evan opened the third one. What he found beyond it was a meek-looking living room. All it had was a small couch, a television, and a lamp cramped together. Could it have been swapped with the bedroom?

Before he could mull it over any longer, faint rustling noises interrupted his thoughts. Jasper must have woken up. That was his cue to leave the hallway behind and see how he was holding up.

Jasper was sitting on the edge of the bed when Evan entered, putting his shirt back on.

"I thought you were already gone."

"I'm not that heartless."

"Ah, why do I somehow not believe you?"

"Right, anyway... It's quite an interesting place you have here." When he got closer to the bed, Evan noticed the rest of his clothes strewn on the floor next to it.

"Aw... I'm being ignored. But, thank you. If that was a compliment, of course. Since you might be taking an interest in 'all of this', I might as well offer you something... Do you want to come with me to an exhibition next weekend? It's new, and I know nothing about the artists, but I love checking out what the creative people around me are making."

Evan listened intently as he got dressed. Art, huh? Sure, he liked Jasper's photography, but that was really it. That world didn't draw him in. If anything, its existence was only a reminder of a critical decision he once made.

"Hmm, I suppose I could be convinced."

"Want a photo?"

That was quick.

"Hmm... alright. As long as you know that I was very close to asking for more."

"Wow, what a kind-hearted businessman you are."

"When did I say what I did for work?"

"Oh, I'm just making assumptions."

"Now, who's the bad guy?"

"Still you."

Evan laughed, as he looked around at the photos around them.

"So, any of these?"

"Yeah."

One of them was constantly getting his attention. There was something about the way the flogger on it was captured that was rather appealing. And it included more of the photographer than most of the others, aka the man standing beside him.

Jasper followed his gaze.

"I see..." He walked up to the wall and gently pulled it off, before speaking up again.

"Good choice."

After handing it over to Evan, he pulled his phone out, still keeping eye contact with him. It took a moment for Evan to process what he was silently asking him for. But once he did, Jasper got the numbers he wanted.

"I'll let you know the time and place later."

"Sounds good... I'll be there. Maybe."

Jasper shoved his shoulder lightly.

"Alright, get out of here already."

"Sure, sure."

With a quick laugh, Evan headed for the door.

"Hold on, I don't think I ever caught your name."

"Don't worry, that happens all the time."

A look.

"It's Evan.

CHAPTER 3

Another day, another trek to the office.

Before leaving, Evan gave the apartment a quick glance. Since he resided inside mostly empty walls, he had no issue getting the photograph up on them.

Looking at it before going to work almost felt like believing in the effects of a lucky charm, with the hopes of at least a bearable workday.

When he got to the office, the suffocating atmosphere clung to him immediately. Same as usual.

Sadly, the first interaction of the day had to be with Erwin. His 'lovely' boss. He offered no greeting, and his gaze only shone with unspoken expectations for Evan.

He didn't say anything new that Evan wasn't already prepared to hear, and yet it still felt grating.

"—That'll be all. You can leave."

The day droned on, and more emails were sent out or received. Some needed his immediate attention because of the damn signature they contained at the end. Erwin.

His lunch break wasn't much better. When he went through the company cafeteria to get his lunch and something to drink, he saw the other employees sitting and making small talk. He didn't pick up on any full conversations, but whatever it was, it sounded very contrived.

At least he was able to take his food to his office, so he could avoid the tense environment. Will even dropped by for a chat.

Unfortunately, that was probably the highlight of the day. And they weren't even that close.

He was often forced to stay late, though luckily it wasn't that bad this time.

Peace was finally within reach. He picked up his belongings and headed out of the building.

Once he was back home, his eyes landed on the same spot they had this morning. A reminder that it wasn't that long until he would be able to meet him again.

It may just be some random art exhibition, but at least it was... something. Anything.

It was early in the evening. The sun was going down, barely visible above the shorter buildings. What did short really mean in a big city like this, though?

In front of some rather unassuming architecture stood a man, leaning against it. He wore exactly what you'd expect to see at this kind of event, i.e., what he always had on. However, the blue shirt was a turtleneck today, which only fit his 'artist image' even more.

Since Evan enjoyed dressing up for occasions like this, he found it appropriate to wear a complete suit. He even had a pair of cufflinks on.

"Look at you... Someone came prepared."

What was meant to be a casual greeting was followed by Jasper keeping his eyes off Evan's with a soft red tint to his cheeks.

"Wait, what's that reaction?"

"Okay... as much as I despise corporate rats and all that, I can't deny I have a thing for suits."

Evan couldn't help but laugh.

"Mhm, I totally get it."

Jasper only responded with a grunt as he pulled the front door open.

"Come—"

"Gladly."

The right corner of Jasper's lips curled up a bit.

"—With me."

Once inside, they were met with tall, colored walls filled with equally tall paintings. It wasn't exactly close to museum-like, but it was still a larger area. The whole place was one room; if the door in the back led to the bathroom and nothing else.

The other people there were gathering in a crowd in front of two people who were setting up to give some form of speech. Jasper went up behind them. He was clearly interested in what they had to say, which was a stark contrast to Evan, whose mind was already wandering.

Thoughts of his office drifted by. The desk and laptop that stood on it... And what about his comfortable bed? It'd be nice to lie in that one right now...

"Evan?"

That took him out of it. Jasper's lips were so close to his ear...

"Uh... yes?"

Jasper smiled.

"They're done talking. But, I mean... If you want to keep standing here, I'm not going to stop you."

"Wait, what did they say?"

"Considering you zoned out like that, I'm guessing you don't actually want to know."

"You already know me so well."

A dismissive wave and Jasper was gone from view. Evan followed after him but at a measured pace. The paintings that surrounded them were of a similar abstract theme, or, as Evan would describe it, 'let's be honest, you just threw paint on the canvas'.

Jasper stopped in front of one of them, searching the wall next to it instead of the painting itself.

"Hmm... No plaque or anything. That's fine, but..."

"So, what's this all about?"

"If you had listened to the speech, maybe you'd know."

"Mhm, but what about this one in particular?"

"Ah, I don't know... Though, hey, hold on. It may not look like it to you, but that is some very intentional brushwork. It definitely means a lot to the one who made it."

"Ah hah, right. And you don't at all feel like this might be a little… pretentious?"

"I see. That's where we're going, is it?"

That started something in Jasper.

"Actually, there's somewhere else I'd much rather go." Evan gestured toward the bathroom door in the back. Jasper's icy expression softened, but not by much.

"Oh, I'll take any excuse right now to shut you up."

"Then all you have to do is follow me."

No one was in there. Yet, at least.

They tried acting as naturally as any two men could while walking into the same stall together.

Once inside, Jasper backed up against the printed concrete, an inviting smile on his lips. If Evan stepped any closer, he'd be fully within his grasp. He was aware of that, yet felt no hesitance.

When he did, Jasper yanked him closer by the tie. Evan's heartbeat spiked from their sudden closeness.

"Ah, hi…"

Jasper huffed. A sudden shove against Evan's shoulder staggered him, as he dropped down to his knees. The tie tightened around his neck, making him choke.

"Hey."

Evan's face was already heating up, but the other man's voice made a shiver run down his spine. He was good…

A clicking sound interrupted them. It came from outside the stall, followed by a heavy dragging noise. Someone was entering.

Their eyes met, but none of them said a word. It was a reminder of where they were, and Evan felt somewhat ashamed of the sick thrill he was garnering from it.

He trailed his fingers up Jasper's thigh before his hand gently cupped the shape that was forming in his pants.

A sharp intake of air and knitted brows. Exactly the reaction Evan wanted.

He felt up the outline that was getting easier and easier to see, still staying above clothes.

"Ah- Mmf."

Close. Too close. Jasper clasped his hand over his mouth, trying to mask his sigh. It was a beautiful sight every time Jasper sucked his stomach in when he put more pressure on his clothed cock. His inhales were deep and shaky, making Evan's lips curve into a smug grin. That was met with a glare and a middle finger in his direction.

He was brought out of the moment when a loud slam came from outside.

A palpable silence hung in the air, which remained even after Jasper had removed his hand from his mouth. The stranger was gone, and yet the tension was stronger than ever.

"So..." Evan's voice was soft, as he slowly unzipped the front of Jasper's pants. With a hesitant smile, he continued.

"You know, I never got to ask you what your situation with testing is. If we're going to continue like this, it'd be good to know." Luckily, as intended, his words were releasing some of the tension.

Jasper's gaze was searching. He was probably debating himself, trying to figure out whether he should humor Evan or reprimand him.

"I'll forgive you... for now. And, yes, all the time. Because, well, you know what I do. You?"

"Regularly. Of course."

Jasper reached his free hand down, combing his finger through Evan's soft hair, as he scratched the back of his head.

"Good boy."

An involuntary moan escaped Evan's lips. His clothes were starting to feel awfully tight and constrictive.

"Oh..."

"Ah, you liked that... Enjoy getting treated like a dog, do you?"

He saw Jasper's knee lift for a split second before something hard kneaded into his crotch. With a needy yelp, Evan grasped the closest thing he could get to. Jaspers shirt.

"Nngh... M- Maybe..."

The man towering above Evan squinted his eyes. He wasn't satisfied with that answer.

"Answer. Don't play coy."

Being clothed was slowly getting more unbearable. But for some reason, it didn't feel like he was allowed to do anything without asking for permission first.

"I- I..."

Evan clawed at the rim of Jasper's pants, as he hesitantly pulled them down alongside his boxers. He got a damn near hypnotic laugh in return. One that was laced with need. Jasper was enjoying this.

"Well?" He pressed down harder on Evan's crotch.

"Fuck... I- I do..."

"There you go." Jasper tightened his grip on the back of Evan's head, making his lips press against the tip of his cock. As Jasper yanked on the tie, Evan felt it breach his mouth, hitting the back of his throat.

His fingers nearly tore through Jasper's shirt.

When he saw Evan shudder from the impact, Jasper loosened his grip again to let him pull away. With a dazed look that made Jasper's face turn a deeper shade of red, Evan lapped his tongue over the glans in front of him.

Evan was completely caught up in the moment as if he had been transported to another place entirely. All he could see—all that was on his mind—was Jasper. And all he wanted to do was please him.

Jasper's legs trembled when Evan took him in his mouth again, as he tried hard not to make a sound.

Once Evan settled into a rhythm, he was encouraged by the hand on the back of his head. Jasper kept scratching him there, while he kneaded his shoe into him. It was all so much stimulation at once; to the point where pre-cum was already darkening his boxers.

That same liquid coated his tongue before Jasper abrasively thrust his cock deep inside. Evan was able to keep up this time though, and pulled away the minute he was able to. He played with the head, dragging his tongue over every inch of it. He even grabbed the base of Jasper's cock and stroked it—fast.

"I- Agh..." Jasper had to step off of Evan to avoid crushing him. The hand on his tie let go as well. He saw it move towards Jasper's mouth as the man pulsed inside him. Jasper was trying to muffle himself, but much to Evan's delight, he could still hear the moan under his breath. Thick liquid followed Jasper's held-back shudder and dribbled down Evan's throat. He grasped Evan's hair tighter, as his thumb traced over his ear.

It was all becoming too much for Evan... He had to reach for the swelling in his own pants.

After only a few seconds of desperately rubbing his restrained cock—his mind went blank.

All he felt was something leaving him, as his body slumped against Jasper's legs.

He clung weakly to the man. Both of them were breathing deeply in the stall's comfortable silence, letting satisfaction settle over them.

"You didn't need much to come, did you?" Jasper let go of Evan's head, using that hand instead to pull everything up and zip his pants.

"Uh, well... It does a lot for me... to get treated like that."

It was a little embarrassing to say out loud. But after what they had just done, it was much easier for Evan to admit.

"Ah, that's actually... uh, let's just leave. I'm not about to let myself get hard again already." Jasper chuckled, though it was a bit shaky.

Evan needed a minute before he was able to stand up.

When he did, their faces got much closer than expected. Neither of them said anything, as they stepped away from the wall. The silence that fell over them this time was a lot more tense. But all they could do was leave the stall.

They tentatively looked around the exhibition hall when they arrived from the bathroom. It was a bit harder to act natural now, but at least one seemed to be looking their way.

"I feel a little bad, so I'm going to go talk to them. You can wait for me outside; I won't be long."

"Sure, I will... sir."

Jasper took in a deep breath, before turning away from him. This was far from over...

Evan watched, as Jasper headed for a booth in the distance. It was manned by the pair everyone had been crowding earlier. After observing them for a minute, Evan left the venue.

When he got outside, he fell back against the cold brick wall. It was getting dark. The night air felt surprisingly soft against his skin after he had gone through such a heated session earlier. A break from getting into a headspace like that was always very necessary.

He could use this time to think back on what he saw back there. Wait, what did he see again?

If an art exhibition didn't mean much to him, then why did he enjoy whatever Jasper was doing? It was all the same to a certain extent, no?

Speaking of that damn photographer, there he was, striding out of the building like he owned the place. This was his element, after all.

"I'm not done with you, Evan."

"Awh, what do you mean? I thought I showed the lovely art in there plenty of appreciation."

"Sure, if you consider the intricate lines—also known as veins—on my cock to be art."

"I mean..."

"Alright, you're coming with me."

Jasper walked right past Evan, not sparing him a single glance. He didn't need to look to know that Evan was going to follow right behind him.

CHAPTER 4

Evan perched on the edge of Jasper's bed, a smug expression on his face. Reciprocating the look, Jasper walked past him to get to the dresser.

"Your room is so moody... In a good way."

Jasper opened one of the drawers.

"Thank you, I think. I did make sure it would feel comfortable here." He pulled out a total of four items, which included lube, condoms, safety scissors, and what appeared to be a roll of electrostatic tape. He was probably used to handling a lot of tools like that since he carried them all with such ease.

"Damn..."

Walking over to Evan, Jasper placed it all down next to him; except for the tape.

"Got a safeword?"

"Right, uh, don't laugh. It's... Basilisk."

"Ooh... You just keep getting cuter."

"...I really need to get a new one."

"No, no, I like it. Keep it."

"Evan smiled faintly to himself.

"Ah, alright. Fine."

"Good good... Also, in case it's ever necessary, you can point to the clock on the wall in whatever way is possible at the time to stop everything. You know, if I feel like muffling you again."

Evan looked behind himself and saw the thing he had made note of the first time he came here.

"Right." When he turned back to Jasper, he was pulling some of the tape out.

"Don't worry, I'll be nice to you today. I can't speak for the future, though. Now... take it off."

Evan watched him carefully as he tugged on his tie, loosening it. After he slipped it off, he threw the slim fabric at Jasper. It landed against his shoulder for a split second, before falling to the floor.

Jasper's cheeks darkened, as Evan unbuttoned his collared shirt in a deliberately slow manner.

"You want me to hurry up, don't you, Jasper?" He dragged his name out.

"...Yes."

Despite the answer he got, Evan kept the same pace going while dragging his shirt off. Jasper squinted his eyes.

"What's with that look?" Evan teased, placing his hands on the rim of his pants. But he stopped again, observing Jasper.

"Evan, please..."

Under Jasper's watchful gaze, his hands almost moved on their own as he hurried to get the rest of his clothes off.

"Sorry."

That lacked any sincerity, and they were both very aware of it.

"Mhm. Watch it."

Jasper leaned closer, wrapping the tape over Evan's chest and around his biceps. He could already feel the pressure, which was making his breath shaky.

"My arms are still feeling pretty free."

When the tape had been tightened, Jasper cut the thin strap off its roll with his scissors.

"For now."

The tape got dragged over Evan's skin yet again; this time it slid under his chest and around the upper part of his forearms.

Once it was cut off as well, Jasper placed his free hand on Evan's shoulder. With a smile, he kneaded his thumb against the man's flushed skin.

"Okay, now you look way too smug."

His smile widened.

"Hah." Jasper pushed him down by the shoulder, which made Evan fall onto his back on the mattress.

"Mmf..." With his cheek pressed against the bed sheets, Evan watched the other man. Jasper took the items over to the nightstand. On it lay a very familiar blindfold. He exchanged the tape and scissors for it.

"I washed it, so there's no saliva on this thing." As Jasper went back to the bed, he brought the cloth close to Evan's face.

"How thoughtful of you."

Jasper pressed the soft fabric over Evan's eyes, gently tying it by the back of his head.

Its darkness enveloped Evan.

Being locked out of one sense, Evan was becoming extremely aware of every sound Jasper made. No matter how loud or quiet it was.

A familiar rummaging sound. He was most likely going through the drawers again.

After a brief moment, Jasper's footsteps got closer. Had he found something?

On instinct, Evan tried moving his arms but was met with harsh resistance.

"Now, now... Lay still, Evan."

A hand wrapped around his arm, holding him roughly down into the bed.

"Ah—"

Evan inhaled deeply as a row of thin spikes—or needles?—traveled across his skin. The prickling sensation made him shiver. The feeling was strange, but it made him feel much hotter than expected.

"Your body is so—ugh... I love the way it reacts to me."

A soft sigh escaped Evan's lips when the spiked wheel trailed down the middle of his chest.

"I... uh..."

After the steel left one part of Evan, Jasper gently caressed that area, before moving it somewhere else. Jasper's touch in those moments felt especially good on his skin. Even the lightest graze of his fingers made Evan quiver in his bonds.

"Shh, you don't need to speak."

The bed creaked, and Evan could feel Jasper's body press down on it. His breathing came from further above, as he traced the spikes along Evan's inner thigh.

The sudden cold contact on such tender skin caused him to shudder. To keep him still, Jasper moved his hand from his arm to his leg.

That made Evan more aware of where Jasper was positioned. He was currently on the bed in between his legs.

Evan gasped as Jasper's row of needles treaded on the most sensitive part of his body.

"F- Fuck..."

It felt dangerous yet pleasurable when it lightly trailed along his shaft. Jasper's breath got closer to his ear, as a wet muscle traced the edge of it.

"Let me feel you..." Jasper whispered, sending a chill down Evan's spine, as his cheeks flared up.

The cold steel left his cock, and not long after, a clinking noise came from the floor. The anticipation the silence brought made Evan inhale deeply.

Jasper was making some sounds he didn't recognize at first. Thinking on it though, there wasn't much it could be other than the condom and lube that he had placed on the bed earlier.

Something soft and slick with a certain substance pressed inside Evan. He wanted to move so badly—more than he was able to. It was starting to get a bit painful. The good kind, of course.

"Nngh..." After all the teasing, it was incredibly relieving to finally feel Jasper in him, even if it was just his fingers for now.

"Mmh... I want you to squirm for me, Evan."

Evan whimpered as all his blood rushed directly to his cock.

Jasper's fingers were replaced with a much larger presence that slowly pushed its way in.

Jasper clasped both of his thighs tightly, burying himself deep within him. Evan arched his back, letting out a desperate moan.

It didn't take long for Jasper to start moving with more rhythm. And every time his hips slammed against Evan's, he went far enough inside to hit his prostate. Evan's moans turned to gasps, as he writhed visibly below Jasper.

Tension was building in him, making his breath catch in his throat. Pre-cum leaked down his cock already.

"Agh- I'm—"

The instant that left him, Evan felt a sudden emptiness. He whined, aware that Jasper was denying him his climax.

He heard wet noises coming from Jasper's direction, as he felt a hand crawl over his face. Jasper was dragging the blindfold off. When it fell down to his neck, he was met with a smug smile. The man was getting himself off, and all Evan could do was watch.

"Oh, I'm sorry. Were you about to come? Ah... I'm afraid that's not going to happen just yet."

All of Evan was screaming to be touched. So much so, that his whimpering was getting quite a bit louder.

"P- Please, Jasper... Let me come..." His voice was weak but full of desperation. Seeing Jasper shudder and moan, as he stroked every last drop out of himself was too overwhelming. It was a striking visual for poor Evan, especially after being blindfolded for so long.

"Ah, hmm... I don't know..."

Evan wrapped one leg around Jasper's back, trying to keep him close. He didn't know what else to do.

"But I- I'm begging you... please..."

Jasper must have seen something in those pleading eyes of his because he suddenly closed his hand around Evan's cock.

"Ugh... You have to stop being so damn cute..." With pre-cum making it easier, Jasper swiftly drove his hand up and down on Evan's shaft.

When the pressure and tension returned, Evan knew he wouldn't be able to take much more.

His eyes shut tightly as he buried his face in the bedsheets. With a heated shudder, his whole body went numb. He felt something leave him, but he didn't have the strength to open his eyes again.

"Jasper..." He couldn't get anything else out, as exhaustion quickly settled in. Dozing off was all he could think of right now, and his body was really favoring that scenario.

"Just relax. I'll take care of everything."

All he could muster was a faint 'you're too good', before his consciousness faded.

"I don't know if you're awake or not, but... well, I guess I hope you aren't. I... thought it'd only be fair to mention that I wasn't too into that exhibition either. That's the only reason I was okay with going to the stall and ending the night early, I promise."

Such a soft voice, accompanied by sunlight seeping through the bedroom's windows. It was just enough to make his eyes open on their own. The only part of him he had the energy to move at the moment.

"Wait... really?"

"Oh, you heard me... I, uh, do want to clarify that that doesn't mean I can't appreciate artists doing what they love. It just wasn't for me."

Evan chuckled weakly, looking around the room. Everything had been cleared up, and they were both covered in bed sheets.

"Mhm... sure."

Jasper sat up, shooting a mild glare in Evan's direction.

"Anyway. You know, I kept thinking about your safeword afterward. Is there a special reason for it?"

It took great effort for Evan to sit up, but luckily Jasper had added another pillow, so there was more to lean against.

"I came up with it because of what I loved doing when I was younger. Sculpt weird creatures."

"Wait, you? You used to be creative? I don't believe it."

"Yeah, yeah, I know. That was just something young me thought would matter. Luckily, I stopped my delusions from getting too far."

Somehow, that felt wrong the instant it came out of his mouth.

"Hmm... Well, I did the exact opposite. I guess all I can tell you is that, look, I'm somehow alive. And I feel great."

Jasper slipped out of bed and headed for his desk. Their eye contact lingered the whole time. Evan didn't know what to say to that; all he did was get out as well. He gathered his clothing as he watched Jasper sit down by his computer.

"You sure do."

Jasper looked over at him, watching Evan with a smile while he put his shirt on.

"Okay, that's not what I meant."

Evan laughed, getting the rest of his clothes back on as well.

He walked over to the chair Jasper was sitting in and drove his fingers through his hair. Jasper sighed, leaning against Evan's hand to feel him more.

"I know, I know. Have fun with whatever it is you do. I suppose I'll see you some other time."

Jasper gently stroked Evan's forearm.

"Go live that comfortable life, or whatever it is you do."

Evan squinted, pressing his fingers a little harder against Jasper's skin. He earned a moan in return, though it sounded purposefully exaggerated.

"Asshole."

Jasper laughed, sitting more upright as Evan's hand left his hair.

"I've got to humble you a bit sometimes."

"Ahah, of course. Bye now, Jasper."

They couldn't keep their eyes off each other while Evan walked away.

It only happened once he left the room, and they weren't physically able to.

What a night...

CHAPTER 5

He hadn't mentioned sculpting to anyone ever since he gave up on it.

But having them brought up again because of someone who didn't abandon his', was making it really hard to bury those nostalgic memories.

"You okay there, Evan? It got kind of quiet."

Oh yeah, he was still there.

Will had been starved for social interaction outside of work and ended up asking Evan to hang out. It wasn't something they did often, but Evan knew exactly how he felt and agreed to it in a heartbeat.

Their day of city exploration was coming to an end. Sadly, the streets didn't offer much for conversation, so Evan was zoning out. Neither had the restaurants, though. Coming up with things to talk to your coworker about wasn't always easy.

"All good, just some personal stuff."

"I see... It is getting a bit late, so maybe we'll end it for today."

They were getting close to some awfully familiar buildings. Now would be an ideal time to split up. These things had to be separated. Work, and... here.

"Sure, man. It's been fun."

"Yeah... Thank you. I think I needed this. Let's always keep in contact, alright? No matter what happens." Will's lip was a bit shaky when he spoke.

"No problem. And, of course, us employees gotta stick together and all that." Evan offered his sincerest smile; however, it took Will a second too long to reciprocate it.

"Right. See you."

"Bye."

And off he went, into the big city crowds.

Something felt a bit off about him. He hadn't been quite himself lately, but Evan didn't have any idea as to why.

It only took a second before his attention was dragged away again. When he ventured down this street, he always felt incredibly comfortable. There was a lot of extra work he had to finish at home, though, so it would only have to be a brisk walk through the area.

At least, that was the plan... But as soon as he rounded the nearest corner, his shoulder bumped against someone else's.

"I'm so sorry." Evan's eyes widened when he saw the person's face.

"It's okay, uh... Evan? Interesting to see you in such a rush."

Just seeing Jasper brought back a ton of mental images.

"Uh... You know... I don't want to get too distracted in this part of town. I have to get home."

"And here I am, not helping whatsoever, huh? I'll leave you to it then."

He was acting so polite; Evan couldn't help but be suspicious.

Jasper was the one distraction Evan couldn't seem to ignore. And he knew, didn't he? The effect he had on him.

"...Wait."

There was that cocky smile.

"Oh, Evan..."

It didn't take even a second for them to survey their surroundings before Evan was pressed roughly against his own wall. Jasper's mouth settled on the crook between Evan's shoulder and neck, as he sucked hard on his soft skin. A low moan escaped his lips, making Jasper's lips curve up.

Evan shivered from the cold air that hit his chest when Jasper successfully unbuttoned the top of his dress shirt.

"Hurry..." Evan's voice was quiet but needy.

"So impatient."

Jasper's chuckle was interrupted by a sudden vibration coming from Evan's pocket.

"Ohh... What were you up to before we bumped into each other?"

"Funny. But I think that's my phone, not a toy."

"You think?"

All Jasper got in response was a smile.

"Sorry, this is probably important." Evan pulled his phone out, feeling Jasper's fingers play along his exposed collarbone. They both saw what word showed up on the lit-up screen.

"It's okay. Your dedication to your master is cute."

"Don't you dare call my boss that ever again."

Jasper laughed and looked around the entrance hall, noticing the door that stood open at the end.

"Well, have fun." Turning in its direction, Jasper headed for the living room. Evan wasn't sure why, but there was something weirdly exciting about having this man stay over at his apartment.

He answered the call and put the phone to his ear, before following after Jasper.

A booming voice came from the other end. Here we go again...

You'd think an expensive apartment like his wouldn't need to mix the kitchen and the living room. But Evan liked the convenience. Plus, the whole room was still massive and modernized. You could tell exactly what was going on.

Evan noticed Jasper eyeing his own photograph. They glanced briefly at each other as Erwin rambled on in the background. He was too damn distracting, that Jasper.

Another hint at the price tag had to be the stairs Evan was making his way to. As he stepped onto it, he could hear mumbling from further away.

"Two floors, huh?" His tone was unclear. Jasper probably didn't know how to feel about it.

"Hey, are you listening?"

"Sorry, Erwin. I am." He peeled his eyes away from the other man and headed upstairs.

The upper floor contained two doors. One of them led to the bedroom, and what he needed was in there.

His laptop sat on the nightstand, begging for him to get back to work. He sat down on the bed and leaned back against the headboard with a sigh. It didn't seem like Jasper followed him, so now all he had was the dim lights and Erwin's 'lovely' voice in his ear. One demand after another.

"Got it?"

"Yeah, but I need to turn on my computer if you want me to do any of that."

The silence was unsettling.

"...Don't. I'm stressed enough as it is. Just get it done."

Beep. He hung up without letting him respond.

Even when Evan wanted so badly to ask him how he thought he felt. He knew Erwin had a lot on his plate, but his tendency to guilt-trip was tiring.

Evan reached for the computer and placed it on his lap.

Though it had been left open, a knock came from the bedroom door. Perhaps Jasper was just being polite.

"Cute place you got here. Nice view of the city too."

"But?"

"What? No. I like it. Though..."

"Mhm." Evan opened the laptop and turned it on. They kept their eyes on each other as Jasper got closer.

"Listen... You know how I feel. But I can still respect that you've worked hard to get all this."

"Thank you, but you don't have to sugarcoat your thoughts. I can take it."

"I swear... If I find out you're into humiliation..."

Evan laughed, patting the empty space on the bed beside him. It took Jasper a moment to realize what that meant, and he eventually climbed onto the mattress.

"Who knows."

Jasper leaned his head on Evan's shoulder with a smile.

"I'm guessing your job's getting in our way right now?"

"...Right you are."

Jasper shifted against Evan's body, getting comfortable. The sounds of the keyboard tapping were calming. It was surprising they were able to sit this close without jumping on each other.

The stillness was getting louder, understandably so. He was becoming increasingly aware of Jasper's presence, as the man's eyes studied every inch of him.

They seemed to linger on his chest. Right where he had forgotten to button his shirt back up.

"How strict are those deadlines of yours?" Jasper's hand was getting awfully close, as he reached over Evan's arm.

Evan was having a tough time keeping his attention on the screen.

"Very, very strict..."

Cold fingers slid under Evan's shirt, making him shiver.

"Awh... that's a shame." Jasper clearly wasn't deterred by that. He kept moving his hand under Evan's clothes and across his skin, as he felt up his chest. When Jasper brushed his fingertips over his nipple, Evan trembled and bit his lip hard to avoid making a sound.

"Jasper..."

With a smile, Jasper slowly pulled his hand back out.

"What?"

Evan gave him a sharp glare before going back to typing. He noticed Jasper disappear from the corner of his eye, only to reappear between his legs the next time he looked up.

"What do you think you're doing?"

"Nothing..."

Cautiously, Evan placed the laptop down next to himself. He could still work like this, though his arm felt a bit strained from it.

Within seconds, Jasper had pulled both his pants and boxers off. Evan was having trouble focusing on the computer once again since his eyes kept drifting to Jasper's hands. He took in a deep breath when the man's fingers played along the inside of his thighs.

The persistent contact made against his incredibly sensitive skin was, well, making its effects visible in front of Jasper. Blood flowed to Evan's cock as it slowly thickened before him.

"Jasper... I'm working..."

Jasper slid a hand up Evan's stomach, proficiently freeing every button on his shirt.

"Yeah?" His hand returned to Evan's thigh, as he pressed his lips to his navel. Tracing up along the ridges of his abs, he saw Evan's arm move in front of his eyes. Evan was fully leaned back now, with his arms resting by his sides. The laptop had been abandoned... for now.

"Incubus..."

Jasper chuckled, as he hovered above Evan, their faces inches from each other.

For a moment, it looked like he was leaning in to kiss him, but he just flashed him a smug grin instead.

Though he wasn't particularly seeking that, he was somehow still irked to have been denied it.

"Oh, Evan..."

"How dare you."

All Jasper did was deepen his smile, as he wrapped his hand firmly around the base of his cock. Evan's head fell further back against the soft headboard. He sighed with need, thankful that some of the tension was finally being released.

Now that there was easier access to Evan's neck, Jasper pushed his lips against his skin. On instinct, Evan reached for the back of his head.

"Mmh... want me to make you come?"

Jasper's low voice made Evan dig his fingers deeper into the man's hair. With a sigh, Jasper slid his tongue up Evan's neck. When Jasper moved his hand along his cock, he deliberately ran his thumb over the frenulum. Evan's eyes closed halfway, his body shuddering, as a heated moan escaped him.

"Ugh... fuck... I- I do... Please—" Evan was disrupted when he felt a sudden pressure against his glans. Jasper had gathered all his attention there, which made every breath he took hitch in his throat.

Hearing and feeling the reaction it was gaining him, Jasper kept teasing him there. Evan felt Jasper's heated cheek against his jaw. Even though Jasper couldn't see much from there, he was still getting worked up.

He sped up his pace and occasionally rubbed the sensitive part under his glans and the frenulum again.

Evan was almost only gasping at this point, his legs quivering visibly. He arched his back, making his lower body shift towards Jasper, searching for more of his touch.

Jasper pulled his head back up, as he watched the other man with satisfaction.

When translucent fluid started forming on the tip of Evan's cock, he shut his eyes tightly.

"There is no visual better than this..." His grip tightened around Evan.

Jasper's words and the almost professional-level handling of his cock was leaving Evan breathless. He couldn't get a word out or open his eyes again.

As Jasper pressed down roughly on him, putting his focus and pressure on the head, the tension that had been building in Evan was released all at once. He whimpered loudly, as his body shook in pleasure.

He felt like sinking into the bed when Jasper worked him until nothing more came out.

He managed to open his eyes halfway and was met with a very self-satisfied man.

"You're... uh... pretty efficient at that..."

Jasper reached over and pulled out the drawer of Evan's nightstand. With a smile, he took out a few sheets of soft paper.

"I try." Bringing them to Evan's stomach, he made sure there were no liquids left on his body. He even dragged his pants back on for him.

"I doubt you have to try that hard."

Jasper chuckled, as he got off the bed. He looked around, before eventually throwing the papers in Evan's trash can.

"...You're too nice. Shouldn't you be working or something?"

"Oh, fuck you."

Getting back into bed, Jasper sidled up beside him, that oh-so-familiar cocky smile on his face.

He was definitely planning on resting there for the rest of the night. Evan could do the same. He could. It was late, and he was feeling exhaustion creep in after their 'activities'. But Evan picked the laptop back up. Just a few more hours...

The next morning arrived way sooner than Evan would have preferred. He was sitting up in his bed, glancing over at the man who stood next to it. Jasper was already fully clothed and checking his phone.

His expression was pensive when he looked down at Evan.

"Me and some friends have an exhibition running at the moment. And yes, I know you didn't care about the other one. But... I thought that since you liked my photography enough to hang it on your wall, you might be a little interested in this one."

"Hmm... an interesting offer. I might take you up on that." Though Evan acted indecisive, he knew he was going.

"Why, thank you, Evan." Jasper put the phone back in his pocket, his expression smug. He then headed for the bedroom door.

"Alright, get out. You've distracted me long enough."

"Now, now. Keep that tone up, and you'll never get any work done. Trust me."

Evan chuckled, not wanting to acknowledge the heat that was spreading across his face.

"Bye now, Jasper..."

With a quick look back, Jasper left the room.

Was Jasper's involvement in the exhibition really enough to make him want to go? Why? It was all so new and confusing.

But somehow Evan was enjoying every moment of it.

CHAPTER 6

A week had passed.

Evan and Jasper ambled through the large doors of the venue's main entrance. Jasper had been giving Evan's suit a few looks but didn't say anything about it. They both knew what was going on; he didn't have to.

Surrounding them were a myriad of art pieces hanging on walls that were specifically constructed for them. The pieces consisted of paintings, photography, and even excerpts of writing printed out and placed in frames. They were all so different, though mostly of an experimental and sexual nature.

"Huh…"

"What? No snarky comment?"

"Don't tempt me."

Jasper smiled, as he led him through the room by the arm.

"Isn't it great, though? So many ideas and messages these people want to get out. I love getting enveloped in all this energy and the different lives of these artists."

"How romantic."

"Okay, not the word I'd use, but fine."

Evan chuckled.

"I mean… I do get what you're saying. Kind of. Maybe."

"As long as I've made you think, I'm happy."

Evan went quiet.

"I… I've been wondering. Why do you want me to understand all of this?"

No response. Jasper had even dropped his arm. He was narrowing his eyes at 'something' behind Evan.

"Gavin?"

Jasper's voice was low. Someone?

Evan turned his head to where he was looking and saw two men heading in their direction.

"Oh, funny meeting you here." One of them spoke up; his tone was sharp. The guy next to him was leaning against his arm.

"At my own event? Yeah, crazy." Jasper visibly tensed up. This man's presence alone was doing something to him.

"Hey now, no need to act like that. I'm here to look at you and your friends' work after all."

Jasper's brows furrowed.

"There's absolutely no need for that. I'll be alright without your filthy eyes on it."

With mock surprise, Gavin turned to the one wrapped around his arm.

"Can you believe that? You're just going to let your friend talk to me like that?"

The guy didn't respond. He only looked apologetically at Jasper.

"Really? You're making your boyfriend stand up for you?"

"He's actually very good at that, you know. Just... when he wants to be. Isn't that right?" Gavin gave the man next to him a pleading look as he leaned closer to him. He completely missed Jasper's point, which was probably intentional.

This time he got a soft smile from him. They got closer, and to only Evan's surprise, locked lips. It only lasted a second, but oh, was it an unbearable one. Jasper rolled his eyes.

"Mhm... And how does my dick taste, Isaac?"

They both stepped away from each other, giving Jasper the hardest glares Evan had ever seen.

That moment made him crudely aware of the fact that he was still there, listening to what was becoming a surprisingly personal conversation.

"You can't just say that." Gavin sounded desperate. Especially so when he saw the man next to him briefly drive his fingers over his own lips.

"Ah? Am I supposed to just forget how much you loved suc—"

"Jasper."

"—king me off."

The silence was palpable, and it first broke when Evan let out a faint chuckle. Gavin gave him a cold side eye, before returning his gaze to Jasper.

"Unbelievable."

"You know, you could just tell me if this is why you broke it off."

He had to think about that.

"...Honestly? Yes. That was part of it. You never shut up."

Jasper snorted.

"Well, I wasn't going to do that any time soon, if ever. So this is for the best."

"Agreed." With a huff and one last look at Jasper, the two pushed past him.

Jasper stayed quiet, finding it a bit difficult to look Evan in the eyes.

"Sorry. That guy brings something out in me."

They finally made eye contact.

"It's okay. I found it kind of funny anyway."

"Phew. Yeah, uh, that was the last guy I've ever had a relationship with. It sure doesn't help that he ended up with my old friend."

"Sounds like a mess."

"It's... not so bad. I just risk running into them at places like this since Isaac sets up exhibitions with the rest of us."

"Fair enough. ...Last ever relationship, huh?"

Jasper glanced off to the side.

"Love didn't end up being for me. I guess it doesn't really fit with my job either."

"Ah..." Evan wasn't too good at responding to such personal information. Never had been.

"We're on the same page about that, right?"

"Yeah."

"Alright... great."

It had been unspoken until now, but there was something nice about putting it into words.

Jasper's attention had been taken once again, and from what Evan could see, it was just one of his own photographs.

Only when Jasper hurried in that direction, did he notice the two people standing in front of it. More trouble was brewing.

But he was too intrigued to not go and see what that was all about.

"Hah, as vile as ever, these are."

"Why are you even here?" Jasper sounded exhausted already. This time it was a man and a woman, who were both a great deal older than Jasper. Evan didn't have to speak to them to know they were the definition of the kind of people Evan expected to see here.

"We just like to support the locals. I'm sure you understand." The woman interjected, sounding incredibly holier than thou.

"How generous of you. I really appreciate it." Jasper's voice was monotone as he looked between the two of them.

"You could learn from some of your more... tasteful friends though."

"I'm not asking for unhelpful criticism. Thank you."

"Tsk. Whore..."

The man whispered under his breath, as the pair passed by Jasper. Evan's eyes widened, but Jasper just smiled.

"You forgot to add 'proud.'"

All he got in response was a huff, and soon they were out of view.

"Ah... how friendly." Evan was being deliberately cautious, not sure what he was allowed to say after that.

"Oh, yeah. It's always a delight to speak to them. But hey, if there aren't some people who don't get it—or even hate it—then it's no fun."

Evan could admire that sentiment. Still, their behavior was branded in his mind.

"That's a good mentality to have. But... there are a lot of elitists like that, aren't there?"

This time, Jasper's glare was directed at him. He got that sinking feeling in his stomach, as the face he had been giving the others all evening was being directed at him.

"You're like one sentence away from asking if all of us are like that, aren't you?"

"Well... I mean... That's all I've ever seen."

"I'm starting to get pretty tired of those comments, Evan. You don't know everything, so stop acting like you do."

"But I'm kind of right, aren't I?"

Jasper didn't respond right away. That was probably the worst thing Evan could have said. Not to mention, Jasper was probably feeling quite tired after those hostile conversations.

"Just... leave. This place clearly isn't for you."

Evan didn't know why that got to him as much as it did. The venue was feeling more and more unfamiliar—claustrophobic.

"I..."

Evan turned around in a rush. He looked back briefly, then headed for the door. There was nothing he could say to that. Nothing.

A few days had gone by since the event.

Evan was sitting in his living room, lost in thought. He watched the cityscape that unfolded outside the room's wide window. Down there, so many stories were being made and told by the minute...

Evan sighed and pulled his phone out. He found the right name, pressed it, and held the overpriced thing to his ear.

"How nice of you to call." Jasper's voice was steeped in sarcasm and apprehension. But he wasn't being outright dismissive.

"Jasper, I'm..."

First now did he realize he had no idea what to even say to him.

"Speechless? Why don't you come over, and I'll fix that for you."

The shift in tone caught Evan off guard. Thinking back on it though, their first time together was initially motivated by some form of anger. So there was a good chance Jasper enjoyed getting his frustrations out that way.

"Are you sure you want to see me right now?"

"Yes."

He didn't need to say more. Evan knew where he was going.

CHAPTER 7

After a few soft knocks on the door, it swung open.

Jasper's expression was unreadable, and he didn't say anything.

"Uh, hi... Jasper."

Without a minute to spare, he pulled Evan inside by the arm and locked the door behind him.

Standing much closer now, Evan could see the man's intense eyes more clearly. He looked ready to slam him against the wall and do it right there, but he didn't.

Seeing the hesitance, Evan placed his hand over Jasper's.

As they stood there, an abrupt bell sound took them out of their tense silence. Jasper retracted his hand, squeezing past Evan to get to the door. When he opened it, he was met with the face of a kind-looking older woman.

"Oh! I'm sorry for arriving so suddenly. It seems like you might be a bit busy."

"That's no issue. It's nice to see you again, Minerva."

Jasper's mood shift was a bit jarring.

"It's good to see you too. But I really wouldn't want to interrupt. How about this? I'll be in town for the week, so come see me when you get the time."

"I'd love to. Just text me the address. You know, the same way you could have told me you were coming."

"I can't surprise my own grandson a little?"

"Ah, alright... I do appreciate the visit."

The woman's smile widened, as she grabbed the door handle.

"That's all I ask. I'll see you soon."

She shut the door, leaving them in silence again. A slightly more comfortable one.

Jasper locked the door with a sigh.

"She seemed nice."

He turned to face Evan.

"Nice? Saint would be far more accurate. She's the only adult who was ever willing to take care of me."

Evan went quiet. Seeing her was clearly bringing back some not-so-pleasant memories for Jasper.

"...I'm sorry about what happened at the exhibition. It was kind of unwarranted."

"At least you understand... I shouldn't have snapped like that either."

"I do need to admit something, though. You saying that the place wasn't for me hurt more than expected. I mean, I shouldn't care about belonging there anyway, right?"

Jasper slipped past him, heading for the bedroom door.

"Well, what do you think? You told me you once wanted this life, didn't you? Or did you just find a little joy in creating something? Either way, I'm sure you have your answer already."

Evan walked up behind Jasper, who was standing in the doorway.

"To be honest... I think I'm a bit jealous of you. This whole world you've gotten into and can somehow live from. It looks so interesting. ...Fun."

"I assure you, it was never easy. Still isn't. You should be happy that you have a good job and get to live comfortably." Jasper paused.

"I often bordered on having nothing at all. It felt like a miracle when I started earning enough from my work. But that doesn't mean I'm well off now. Far from it. It's a life of uncertainty."

Evan knew he was right. He had been told that many times in the past. And yet...

"You really enjoy it though, don't you?" Evan trailed his fingers up under Jasper's shirt, making him shiver.

"I... yeah. Despite everything, there's nothing else that could make me feel this good. The art and the people I get to meet... it makes it all worth it." Jasper leaned back, letting the other man's body support him.

Evan smiled, sliding his hand further up. He loved the way Jasper's muscles tensed.

"Exactly..."

Jasper abruptly grasped Evan's arm, a heated look in his eyes.

"This time... I want you to fuck me."

That was not what he expected to hear. But damn if it didn't make him feel something. He liked it both ways, after all.

"You'd give me the honor?"

Jasper chuckled, pulling Evan's hand out. He then released his arm and stepped forward.

"I don't want to think right now... Make me forget it all."

Evan watched Jasper carefully as he yanked his shirt off and threw it to the floor. Seeing Jasper like this was familiar, but there was a hint of something else. Something new.

"I could never say no to that..."

Throwing his own shirt to the floor as well, Evan walked closer. He traced the harness Jasper still wore, slipping a finger under the longest strap that crossed his chest.

"Want me to take it off?"

Evan tugged at it with a smile. He then let go, making it slap against Jasper's skin. A melting sigh left him.

"No. It looks good on you..."

Jasper's cheeks darkened, as he got down onto the bed, and ran a hand over his own thigh.

"Come get what you want then, Evan..."

If the sight of him feeling himself up wasn't powerful enough, then that was officially his cue to ravage the man.

Evan crawled over Jasper, pushing him down by the shoulder.

"How is it that every other day I want to be completely broken by you, but tonight I feel the exact opposite?"

Jasper reached for the back of Evan's head and held him close.

"Let's just say... I always know what men want. No matter the situation." He snuck his other hand in between Evan's legs, sliding his fingers over his clothed cock.

Evan struggled to stay still above him. His lips trembled, trying to conceal a moan.

"Mmh... fuck... Yeah, you do..." With slight difficulty, Evan kneaded his knee into Jasper's crotch.

Seeing the man shudder beneath him, a pleased smile parted Evan's lips. He dug his fingers into Jasper's hair, gripping it firmly by the root.

Jasper gasped, his strength failing him, as his arms fell back down onto the mattress.

Satisfied, Evan looked over at the nightstand, where the lube and remaining packets from last time still stood.

He gathered what he needed with his free hand and placed it on the bed.

"You're taking too long..."

Jasper whimpered, grinding his lower body against Evan's knee. If this kept going, Evan wouldn't be able to control himself much longer.

"Huh, why do I still feel like making you wait?"

"Evan..."

He held Jasper's hair tighter, yanking it down, as he practically crushed his cock with his leg.

"Yeah?"

A shaky whine escaped Jasper.

"Fuck... you..."

With a laugh, Evan let him out of his grip, placing both hands on the rim of Jasper's pants. It was about time...

It didn't take long to get them both out of their clothes. He would love to keep teasing Jasper, but he was getting quite impatient himself.

After smearing some lube on his fingers, he pushed the cold liquid gently inside Jasper.

It didn't mean he couldn't go a little slower than usual, though. Just to mess with him.

Jasper pressed his lips tightly together.

"Let me hear you, Jasper..."

"Not if you... keep stalling. I want you inside me..." His voice was almost hypnotizing.

Evan had to pause for a moment to mentally refresh after that. He dragged his fingers back out and reached for the bottle next to them.

"God... I love you."

As Evan rolled a condom on with the lube, he noticed Jasper giving him a certain look. He had to follow that up, didn't he?

"Not like that."

Jasper laughed but was abruptly cut off when Evan, with a sudden thrust, breached his body.

"Agh— Yes! Finally..."

Evan pulled him closer by the hips, making Jasper choke on air as the head of his cock hit against his prostate. Being fully enveloped by Jasper felt so good that he impulsively moved inside him with needy thrusts.

To gain some control back and to feel Evan more, Jasper threw one of his legs over his shoulder. Evan's eyes widened at first, but it didn't hinder him. He let out a huff, as both of his hands slid down Jasper's thighs. With a smug grin, Evan got a good grip on his ass.

"Good enough for you, Jasper?" Evan shoved himself to the hilt inside Jasper as he groped him.

"Nngh— No. Harder."

Evan had to wonder if Jasper knew exactly how he made him feel.

"Ah, good answer..."

Evan returned his left hand to Jasper's hair while he slapped his ass hard with the other. Jasper yelped, and his body arched visibly.

At last, Jasper's thirst had been satiated.

His moans were so sweet, as he squirmed and quivered with every thrust or slap against his bare skin. Pre-cum leaked down Jasper's cock, which Evan felt slick his own as well.

When he checked to see how red Jasper's skin was getting, a desperate whimper came from his direction.

"I- I... fuck... I'm—"

Evan trembled when Jasper suddenly tightened around him. With such a beautiful man writhing in pleasure beneath him, Evan couldn't possibly hold himself back anymore.

He shoved himself as deep inside Jasper as he could, which made a strong surge course through his body. Letting out a heated moan, Evan came. He had to place both hands on the bed to stabilize himself.

Evan drew his cock out of Jasper, as he let the man's leg fall down onto the mattress. Their eyes connected, exhausted grins on their lips.

Breaking away from it momentarily, Evan glanced beside the bed, knowing exactly where to dispose of the rubber.

Once it was thrown away, he leaned his head down between Jasper's legs.

"I could get used to seeing you like this..."

Jasper didn't say anything. He just took in a shaky breath and watched Evan with half-lidded eyes.

Evan trailed his tongue over the opaque liquid that was dispersed across Jasper's abdomen and inner thighs. His breath hitched when Evan came into contact with his cock, but he stayed quiet otherwise. Evan was enjoying the unspoken tension.

He did move away eventually, though. Since Jasper had pretty much been licked clean, he was out of excuses to keep going.

Evan nestled into the bedsheets next to Jasper. He couldn't be bothered to move the extra packet or the bottle, though he had just enough energy to pull the covers over them.

A comfortable silence hung in the air as Jasper absentmindedly grazed his fingers over Evan's chest.

"It still burns. I love that feeling..."

Evan snuck a hand under Jasper's body. He grabbed his ass roughly, digging his fingers into his soft skin.

Jasper couldn't conceal a gasp of surprise in time, and with a soft whine, he buried his face in Evan's neck.

"Who's cute now?" His hand remained clasped on Jasper, making the man shakily clutch his chest.

"You. Still you."

Evan chuckled and let go of him, deciding to wrap his arm around Jasper's waist instead.

"Fine... I guess I'm gonna have to accept that label at this point."

"Good. Took you long enough."

He rolled his eyes, holding Jasper tighter to himself.

"There was, uh, something I wanted to ask you back at the exhibition."

"Oh?"

"I was just curious as to why you're so determined to, I guess, prove art to me."

"Right... that. Honestly, I'm not sure. Maybe I'm hoping to turn a skeptic around to it. You know, because trying that with my family wasn't exactly working out."

Evan didn't know what response he could possibly come up with for that, which was becoming pretty common with this guy.

"Huh... I see."

"Yeah, I know. It's a bit ridiculous."

"No... I wouldn't say so. I'd probably have done the same if I were as convicted and passionate as you."

Jasper went quiet. He smiled to himself, but he was also trying to keep it subtle. As he caressed Evan's chest, he moved his body as close to him as possible.

"You can be really charming when you want to. Ugh, just... fall asleep already."

"As you wish, sir..."

As a deep red spread across Jasper's cheeks, he growled dismissively and closed his eyes.

Evan buried his face in the man's hair. With a satisfied sigh, he followed suit and dozed off as well.

CHAPTER 8

Evan was sitting in his office when it happened.

Erwin personally came to the door instead of Will. His eyebrows drew together, and his lips were in a straight line, which conveyed nothing.

"Come to my office. Now."

He left as quickly as he came.

Evan wanted time to digest that. To consider what was happening. But it would be bad to leave him hanging...

It took a few minutes to get there.

The silence in his boss's grand office was as unnerving as always.

"I don't enjoy having to tell you this, but I know you two talk occasionally. So, I thought it would be best to notify you myself."

Evan walked closer, eyes intently on Erwin's. He continued.

"There's something more relevant to you as well, so please stick with me. ...Will doesn't work here anymore." He opened his mouth to speak again but stopped himself when he saw the way Evan trembled.

No way. He was the only person Evan could talk to at work. What now?

"Why...?"

"I'm sorry. I can't give you that information. But, listen, there's something else. Though you might be a little snappy—perhaps for good reason—you've been very diligent ever since we hired you. Because of it, I've been considering offering you a promotion. Actually, I am."

The whiplash was making Evan's head spin.

"I..."

"I'm sure you're aware of the pros and cons."

An opportunity to work closely with this man and the chance of really making it somewhere. That included wealth, of course.

But his free time would be nonexistent. Would he be able to spend any time with Jasper if that happened?

Also, there would be no coworker to make every day a little less tiresome.

He couldn't. There was no way he was letting go of the new world he had discovered.

"I am aware. And I don't think I can accept your offer. If possible, I'd like to keep working like I am now." He was trying to still maintain some professionalism.

Erwin didn't say anything at first. He merely studied the employee who stood in front of his desk.

"Alright. If that's what you want." It wasn't clear whether he approved of Evan's decision or not. But when were his thoughts ever obvious?

He spoke up again.

"That's all. You can go now."

With a dismissive wave of Erwin's hand, Evan left the office.

It wasn't any less suffocating in the halls of the company building, despite most of it being made of glass. He wanted so badly to just leave and go home for the day. But after that meeting, it would only be right for him to keep proving himself to his boss.

The walls trapped him inside for yet another day.

Feeling lost even during the weekend, Evan wandered around his apartment. It was all spiraling in his head.

His coworker getting fired or quitting... The decision he still wasn't sure was the right one...

He had to consider what really mattered to him if he wanted these grueling days to end.

A thought crossed his mind.

Of course.

He marched to the entrance hall and threw his jacket on.

It was time to go back. But first, on to the store.

A few hours later, he came staggering into the apartment, a myriad of items in his arms. It was a bit tough to lock the door, but he managed.

Bringing it all to the living room table, he sat down on the couch with a sigh. Clay, a plywood board, and some shaping tools.

Eating here might be difficult from now on.

The clerk gave him some pointers when he was out, so getting back into the process of this wasn't going to be too foreign.

Evan got to work.

It was surprisingly freeing to sit there and mold that little clump of nothing into... something. It didn't look like much even as time went on, but Evan didn't mind.

It was simple and fun. A reminder of how he used to do it every chance he got in art class and such. Until it became a waste of time. At least, according to him at the time.

Minutes turned into hours.

He took a moment to just look at it. Squinting his eyes, he could kind of imagine it looking like a dragon head. Kind of.

Caught up in the excitement, Evan picked up his phone.

All he told Jasper over the phone was to come over, but for some reason, he didn't ask any questions and just agreed to it. Was it the tone of his voice?

It was getting late when a knock came from the entrance.

Evan hurried to get to it and found a man standing in anticipation beyond the door.

"So... What's going on with you?"

"I, uh..."

What he hadn't prepared for was the embarrassment that slowly crept in from having to tell Jasper about it.

"Well?"

"Just... follow me."

They walked into the living room together. When Jasper saw what was standing on the table, his eyes immediately lit up.

"Oh! Wait, you did it. I'm not sure if that's supposed to be some sort of reptile, but it's cute."

Evan rolled his eyes, but his smile was impossible to erase.

"Is it weird for me to be excited about this? Somehow I can't stop calling myself childish."

"I get why you might think that. But in our stressful lives, it's pretty important to remind yourself to have fun. You know, remember what fun even means. The communities I joined kept telling me that, and I couldn't agree more."

"Hmm..."

"Also, there's no need to worry about getting far with art if you don't want to. That never has to be your end goal."

"You have a lot to say about this, huh?"

Jasper chuckled as he slipped into the couch.

"Why yes, I do. It's my life after all."

"Well, you're probably right, my clever and experienced artist."

"I'm yours now, am I?"

"For tonight, maybe..."

Jasper leaned back on the couch. His smile was... inviting.

However, when thoughts of his talk with Erwin resurfaced, he couldn't make a move.

"Is something wrong, Evan?"

"The only coworker I ever got to talk to on a more personal level got fired. Or quit. I don't know..."

"Have you talked to them about it?"

"No..."

Jasper didn't need to say more. His intense gaze said enough. Evan spoke up again, determined.

"Should I do what your grandma did? I doubt he'll open up if I just call."

"If you know he'd be okay with you showing up at his door all of a sudden."

"That shouldn't be a problem."

"Off you go, then. Leave me and my new apartment alone."

Evan smiled.

"Alright, alright, have fun."

As Evan walked through the hall leading to the door, he glanced back at Jasper through the doorway. He was looking at the clay with a smile, which Evan immediately took to heart.

He made the right choice.

When Evan showed up at his coworker's door, he was met with a look of surprise. It quickly turned into one of realization, though.

"...Evan. I was going to tell you. I was."

Evan wrapped his arms tightly around him.

"Please don't apologize; I'm sure you had your reasons. And... you were never obligated to tell me about it."

It took him a moment, but he eventually reciprocated the hug.

"Thank you... I may have gotten fired—abruptly, I might add—but I got in once. I'll get in again. Somewhere else. You don't have to worry about me."

Evan retracted his arms. He knew as much, but that didn't mean Will was going to be fine with all of this.

"I at least want to make sure you know I'm here for you."

Will sighed, before stepping back into the entrance.

"Want to come in?"

That would be the first time Evan had even set foot inside his house.

"I'd love to."

It was going to be a quiet night. But a much-needed one.

CHAPTER 9

"Make one of those little sculptures for me."

"Don't you hate it when people demand you take photos for them?"

"Uh... please?"

Evan was sitting on the edge of Jasper's bed, as the two enjoyed another evening of each other's company.

"Okay, I'm going to need more than that."

Jasper was currently at his desk in the corner of the room.

"I want to show some of my artist friends what you've made. I might have told them some things..."

"Ah, I see. Not too much, I hope."

"Just that I've met this guy who swore off art but then eventually came back to it."

"I suppose that's alright. How do you plan on showing it to them?"

"We're having a gathering to show off our progress and finished projects. I've been meaning to invite you, but I want to get your work in there too."

"Hmm..."

"Also, enough with that formal talk. I'm getting a little worked up..."

Evan moved back on the bed with a smug grin.

"Really, now? Then I have an offer for you. Do a rough scene with me this time. And I'll consider it."

"I hope you know that that's only beneficial for me." Jasper got out of the chair and towered over Evan, who was still sitting down.

"Then why am I not screaming already?"

Jasper's smile widened.

"I'll see what I can do about that." Walking up to the black slate on his wall, Jasper pulled a long hank of rope off one of the hooks.

Evan watched as he brought it back to the bed with him. He moved further back on the mattress once they were face-to-face again.

"Looks like the soft kind. Nice."

"Mhm. Put your wrists together."

"What? No small talk?"

Evan acted smug, but he still did as he was told. Leaning down until his back hit the mattress, he raised his arms over his head.

"Weren't you the one hurrying me a second ago? Or are you just being difficult on purpose?" Jasper crawled onto the bed, his knee placed in between Evan's legs, dangerously close to his crotch.

He untangled the rope and slowly wrapped it around Evan's wrists.

"Oh no, he's catching on."

Jasper chuckled, lacing the rope over itself in the opposite direction to tighten it. Evan shifted against the sheets, testing its strength. It proved fairly difficult to move much more than his lower body, which was surprisingly arousing.

Jasper took the scissors that still lay on the nightstand and cut the rest of the rope off, before putting it back again. He then tied the ends into a knot and ripped Evan's shirt open.

It only took a few minutes before the last fabrics covering him were gone as well. It all made him feel so vulnerable, especially when Jasper's hungry eyes scoured his exposed body.

"I have a question, Evan." He got off the bed and headed for the hooks once again.

"Yeah?"

His dresser stood below them. Dragging the top drawer out, Jasper rummaged through it. He pulled out an object that Evan discerned as a toy shaped to enter someone and a riding crop.

He placed both on top of the dresser, but his hand hovered over the long, thin one.

"How did you feel about artists again? You know, before you met me?"

Evan caught on to where this was going, and he was more than willing to go along with it.

"Oh, hmm, I don't know... That they're all self-righteous and up their own asses?"

Jasper clutched the handle of the riding crop and turned around. As the soft end of it traced down the middle of Evan's chest, he inhaled deeply. Knowing what came next was making his heart race.

"Awh, that's not very nice..."

"Did that cut a little too dee—Agh!"

Stinging pain carved itself into Evan's lower waist, making his body jolt. Jasper watched him—pleased—as he stroked the same spot with his hand.

"Did that?"

Though Evan was trembling, a smile crept onto his face.

"Mmh... could have gone harder."

Without giving him a second to breathe, Jasper slammed the whip against his skin yet again. Evan's sharp inhale shifted into a moan right at the cusp, as he writhed against the bedsheets.

"Look at you... Getting hard just from this. What a slut." Jasper picked up the other toy with his free hand, and when he pressed his finger into a specific part of the base, a clicking noise sounded, and it started buzzing. He brought it closer to Evan's lower body, which made his legs twitch in response.

"S- Says... you..."

When Jasper pressed it to the head of Evan's cock, a needy moan escaped him. The speed of that toy's vibrations caught him off guard, and its contrast from the pain was startling.

"Behave, Evan."

Jasper only wanted to give him a taste of pleasure before he eventually took it away again. Now that nothing was touching him anymore, Evan let out a whine.

"I'm sorry. I will... just... Let me feel it again."

"Good boy." Jasper drove it up along the underside of Evan's shaft, meanwhile circling the end of the riding crop around his nipple. It felt like he was melting into the bed as he shifted against it.

His moans were steeped in desire, hitching in his throat when Jasper whipped his chest with a controlled grip.

"Jasper, please... fuck me... I want you..." Evan, through blurred vision, saw the other man's eyes widen momentarily.

"Patience..."

Jasper didn't act upon how it made him feel, though.

"But—Nngh..."

The toy dipped down below Evan's cock, grazing his perineum.

"I suppose you've earned this."

Jasper leaned down and spat on the black silicone, before shoving it brusquely inside him. Since it wasn't covered in lube, the pain that accompanied his actions made Evan whimper loudly. His throat felt dry, but... he loved it.

Everything around them was fading away. It was just him and Jasper in the void now. The red, dimly lit void this room had become. As tears kept crowding his eyes, his body shuddered from the vibrations that came into contact with the gland deep within him.

Leaving his toy inside Evan, Jasper put the riding crop back into the drawer. He then got a hefty-looking flogger off its hook.

Jasper watched him with a smile, before trailing the multi-stranded whip over Evan's body. He quivered from the different sensations hitting him all at once.

When Jasper whipped that same leather multiple times against his chest and abdomen, Evan cried out in ecstasy, his back arching with every lash. A familiar surge was making itself known inside him.

"I- I...!"

Evan's eyes widened, and his mouth shut tight the instant he heard himself. He had been reminded of what happened last time, but it was too late.

With a cocky expression, Jasper let the flogger fall down onto the bed next to Evan and forced the vibrator out.

"Don't think I'm letting you come before I've had a proper taste of you."

Evan whined, pulling on the rope. It didn't give whatsoever, and Jasper merely chuckled at him. As he got his clothes off, he remembered to leave a certain piece on.

Seeing Jasper like that only made Evan long for him even more.

"Yes, please... Give it to me..."

Jasper didn't respond at first, but the red on his cheeks spoke for him. Keeping eye contact with Evan, he prepared himself with the rubber and lube.

Once Jasper finally crawled onto the bed, he hovered above him as they both took in a deep breath simultaneously.

"Ah... you're too good, Evan..."

Evan shivered as Jasper's hands closed around his thighs with a tight grasp. He pulled him closer, and with a huff, breached Evan's body. It was an indescribable feeling—the way the warmth of Jasper's rigid cock filled him up.

The violent thrusts that followed nearly made him choke, while heated moans left him every time Jasper went as deep as he could.

An intense surge of pleasure coursed through his body once more.

With a particularly harsh thrust, Jasper buried his cock deep in him. All tension and pressure released at once, as Evan's breath hitched high in his throat, and his body convulsed.

He couldn't keep his eyes open any longer. Though he sank into the mattress in satisfaction, it still felt like he was floating.

It wasn't often he reached this state, but the high was like its own form of spiritual experience.

Something soft ran over Evan, removing the liquid that clung to his skin. After Jasper's touch left him, he heard the man rummage around the bedroom. Evan was unable to move his body, so when Jasper untied the rope, he also helped him get his arms back to his sides.

Evan finally managed to open his eyes again. What appeared before him was Jasper's gentle expression, as he pulled extra covers out from under the bed. He laid them over both of their bodies, wrapping Evan securely in their warmth.

"I... uh..."

Evan wasn't sure why he even tried to speak, knowing full well it would be completely incoherent.

"I've never met anyone this receptive to me. How could I possibly ask for more... You can't respond right now; I know. You don't have to."

Jasper grazed his hand over the red marks scattered across his skin. All Evan could do was smile as he curled up next to the other man.

It was a staggering compliment, but Evan couldn't quite get his thoughts together. The only thing he knew at that moment was that this, this was what pure bliss felt like.

An unexpectedly grandiose house stood before them.

They had driven far out of the city, to what could be considered a mountain or a hill, depending on where you came from.

The clearing they stood in was covered in a canopy of trees, as foliage spread out around them. A house like this in such picturesque isolation was certainly a spectacle.

"Nice, huh? We all chipped in to rent this place out for the weekend. We get to have our own little exclusive gallery."

"Yeah, wow. Wherever you ended up putting my 'thing', it definitely didn't deserve to be."

"Oh, shut up. It's the reason it exists that matters."

"Yeah, yeah. Let's go in."

Jasper strolled up to the large front door, still glancing back at Evan with a grin.

"You already know exactly what that attitude is going to get you."

"Correct. That's why I do it."

Jasper held the door open for him.

"Get in."

"Of course, sir... Anything for you."

Jasper tried to mask the way that made him react, but Evan noticed.

This wasn't the time for it, but teasing Jasper was way too fun.

The evening went on, as Evan explored the mansion-like venue. Many different pieces grabbed his attention, but Jasper's still held it the longest.

His own clay creature stood close to that man's photos, which made him feel something... indescribable.

Evan didn't dare try to make a dragon head this time. He had gone for a snake instead. A much simpler shape that he was much more confident with. Even if it wasn't anything special.

Some of Jasper's friends came up and gave him a few compliments on it, but he could tell they were mostly being polite.

That became more evident as some also mentioned how Jasper had told them the story behind it. Some of it.

None of that mattered, though. Evan was satisfied. This whole scenario felt unreal to begin with; there was nothing more he could ask for.

Eventually, he broke off from the excitement and searched for peace in the house's garden. A few people were hanging out in the moonlit greenery, but everyone seemed a lot more laid-back here.

Evan wasn't used to all that energy, since his life had always been swallowed up by silence.

A bench was standing by itself, hidden further in the back of the garden. Perfect.

He went over to it and sat down with a long but satisfied sigh. A lovely visual spread out in front of him. The cold light outside contrasted with the soft, warm glow coming from the building's windows.

Also, the back door. Someone was coming out of it. And he was headed right in his direction.

"Enjoying the night air?"

The one who made all of this possible.

"Yeah… it's so relaxing out here. I mean, I love city life and all, but this has its own charm."

"I know, right? It helps with inspiration, too. At least for my friends. The nightlife I'm indebted to will always inspire me the most."

Evan chuckled as Jasper sat down beside him.

"…Thank you."

Jasper's eyes landed on his.

"For?"

"Ah… well… Man, this isn't easy for me."

"Thanking people? Ugh, you're being cute again."

"Shut up… Jasper, I can't express how great it is to have met you. You're too good for me."

Jasper's eyes opened further. He definitely didn't expect something so passionate. And perhaps a little sappy.

"Woah now… If you want me to fuck you, you can just ask."

Evan rolled his eyes and, with a smile, scooted closer to him.

"Hey, I'm being serious."

"I know, I know. Thanks for telling me. I'm glad I've actually helped out in some way. It's nice to see people give the other side a chance. 'Someone' could have learned a lot from you."

"If… your family never comes around to it. I hope you know you can always come to me."

"Ah… fuck you…" Jasper leaned back, making the wood creak, as he glanced off to the side. Tears were gathering in the corners of his eyes, and it took a second for him to be able to look at Evan again.

"Awh, but it's healthy to show your emotions."

"I will not be hearing that from you, mister businessman."

Evan laughed as Jasper's shoulder landed against his.

"Come on. At least I'm not as bad as my boss."

"I don't doubt that."

Neither of them could stop smiling. Evan felt completely tranquil at that moment. Everything was exactly as it should be. All he ever needed was right here.

Jasper, a beautiful environment, passionate people, and the hope that he so desperately needed.

"Should we go back inside? There's some pieces I want to take another look at."

Jasper's face lit up.

"I'd love nothing more."

Maybe this world wasn't all that bad...

This man was in it, after all.